Look at Chameleon!

by Cynthia Rothman
illustrated by Jason Wolff

Table of Contents

The Best Lizard

Chameleon was a cute little lizard. He always played well with the other lizards.

He liked a lot of lizard games. He liked to jump up and down. He liked to play tag.

One day, the lizard friends sat by a pond.

"I am the best lizard of all," said Yellow Lizard. "I can hide in the yellow sunlight."

"You are not," said White
Lizard. "I am the best lizard
of all. I can hide in a field
of white flowers."

"You are not," said Green Lizard. "I am the best lizard of all. I can hide in the green grass."

"You are not," said Brown
Lizard. "I am the best lizard
of all. I can hide in the
brown earth."

Lizards Together

Everyone looked at the spotted Chameleon. He did not speak.

Then something happened.
"Look at Chameleon!" said
Yellow Lizard. "Now he is
yellow. He can hide in the
yellow sunlight."

"Look at Chameleon!"
said White Lizard.
"Now he is white. He
can hide in the white
flowers."

"Look at Chameleon!"
said Green Lizard.
"Now he is green.
He can hide in the
green grass."

"Look at Chameleon!"
said Brown Lizard.
"Now he is brown.
He can hide in the
brown earth."

The lizards left Chameleon.
They needed to talk.

Soon they came back. "We think you are the best lizard of all," said Yellow Lizard. "You can hide anywhere!"

"Well," said Chameleon. "I think you are the best lizards. You can each hide in a special place."

"We can!" they said.

And all the lizards jumped up and down. They were very happy!

Comprehension Check

Retell the Story

Use a Character Chart to help you retell about Chameleon and his friends.

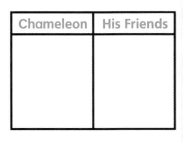

Chameleon	His Friends

Think and Compare

1. Why is the setting important to the story of Chameleon?

2. All of the characters in the story can do something special. What makes you special?

3. Think of a group of animals. Tell what is special about them.